HIT-N-RUN MURDER

MIAMI SLICE COZY MYSTERIES, BOOK 3

PATTI BENNING

SUMMER PRESCOTT BOOKS PUBLISHING

CHAPTER ONE

"There is no way she's going to check for dust up here," Sonja complained from where she was standing on top of a step stool, running a dusting wand along the top of a register that was set near the ceiling.

"I'll know it's there, though," Cassie replied. She was at the counter, counting out the cash before they opened. She'd already put in a good hour of cleaning herself and didn't feel very bad at all for her employee, who had just arrived fifteen minutes before. "Plus, every little bit helps if we want to make a good impression."

"It will be kind of cool to meet her," Sonja admitted, climbing down from the step stool "I haven't met the actual boss yet." She looked at Cassie and hesitated. "Not that you're not my boss, but … well, you know…"

"I know," Cassie admitted with a laugh. "I've only met her once myself, so I get it. That's why I am so concerned about making sure the restaurant is clean. We've got to make a good impression on her."

"Well, she won't be able to complain about the place not being clean. I think that's it for this room. I'll go see if Doug needs help." She ducked into the cleaning closet to drop off her supplies, then went into the kitchen where Cassie heard her running water and chatting with Doug, who was on cooking duty, getting the by-the-slice pizzas ready for the early lunch rush.

The special this week was a classic Chicago-style deep dish pizza. There weren't any fun twists when it came to toppings this time, but Cassie had had to go out and buy special pans just for the special, so she figured it was probably enough of a difference from their normal offerings to count. The layers of cheese and tomato sauce in the deep, flaky crust was decadent, and even though yesterday had been their first day offering it, it was already one of the most popular specials they'd had since she had started there.

Still, the pies took a longer time to cook than usual, and she'd spent all day Saturday showing her employees how to make them, so it had been a rather time-consuming special so far. The fact that she'd had to spend a few hours Friday evening watching YouTube videos and experimenting in her own kitchen was something that she wasn't about to share with them. Cassie might run a pizza restaurant, but that didn't mean she was a talented cook. Sometimes she envied people with natural skill in that department, but she figured she shouldn't complain too much; she might not have a gut instinct for it like some people did, but she could follow a recipe, and she enjoyed it well enough.

Though, with Ellie flying in later, Cassie was beginning to regret her choice for the week's special. She would have preferred to showcase one of her more unique creations to her boss. She still had the idea for a sushi pizza in the back of her mind, but worried that might be a bit too far off the beaten path for what was a very traditional pizzeria.

She sighed, putting the cash back in the register and writing down the amount. Then she glanced at the clock and leaned back in her chair, glad to have a short break before she had to unlock the doors and begin the day. She loved her job, she really did, but she had gotten used to being the head honcho around here. She wasn't dreading Ellie's visit, exactly, but she was … wary about it. Would her boss want to change the way she'd been doing things? Had she been doing things wrong this whole time without realizing it? It wasn't as if she couldn't take criticism, she would just … rather not have to.

Her phone buzzed and she checked it to see a text from Bridget, her sister. Bridget had come to live with her a few months before, after dropping out of college unexpectedly, and had only recently found a job. It was at a small, corner grocery store that was only a few blocks from Cassie's apartment, and thanks to the discount she got, Bridget had become the one in charge of their groceries. The responsibility was definitely a new experience for her sister, but it was doing her good. Bridget was only supposed to stay with her for a month, but the arrangement had turned into a long-term one without either of them really discussing it. Especially now that Bridget had a job, Cassie wouldn't have felt right kicking her out. As long as her sister kept making baby steps forward, Cassie wasn't going to complain. She felt closer to Bridget than she ever had in the past; the ten years between them had meant they were never very close growing up.

The message her sister had sent her was a picture of a shopping basket full of cheese. Following it was an eye roll emoji and a message that read, *Since you cleaned out the fridge Friday night.*

Grinning, Cassie typed out a quick reply. *Come on, we don't need that much cheese. Plus, we've got pizza for days now. We're not going to need cheese for anything any time soon.*

The reply came a moment later. *Yeah, three weird, lopsided pizzas that all have the exact same toppings. I'm really looking forward to eating those for the next week.*

Cassie blushed and tucked her phone in her pocket, deciding to ignore her younger sister's sarcasm. They'd already eaten the fourth pizza that she made, and Bridget had a point. She wasn't exactly looking forward to eating nothing but Chicago-style deep dish pizza for the next week either.

Someone tried to open the door only to find it locked, and Cassie looked up to see a very familiar face on the other side of the window; Antonio. He met her eyes through the glass and raised an eyebrow, glancing back down at the door handle. She checked the clock, saw that it was a minute past eleven, and scrambled to go unlock it. Of course, for him, she would have opened the door anyway, but she hated the fact that she'd been so distracted that she had opened late. It wouldn't have been a good look if Ellie was there.

"Hey, you're here early," she said, welcoming him in. Antonio worked as a security guard at the bank just down the street that the pizzeria used, and she'd met him a few months before. He had quickly become one of her closest friends, and she couldn't deny that there was a deeper attraction there as well. Sometimes, she even thought that he felt the same way, but neither of them had made a move to change the nature of their relationship yet.

"Rossi wanted to get lunch with his girlfriend later, so I decided to trade breaks with him." Antonio inhaled deeply, looking around. "It smells great in here. Do you have any slices ready to go yet? If not, that's fine. I mostly just wanted to say hi."

"They should be coming out in just a second," she said, glancing back toward the kitchen. An idea occurred to her. She looked back at Antonio slyly. "Do you like deep dish pizzas?"

He blinked. "Yeah, I like pretty much any pizza."

She grinned. Once again, Antonio had come to her rescue, and he didn't even know it yet. Bridget was going to be thrilled. "Well, I was experimenting at the apartment the other night, and I may have made too many pizzas for just Bridget and me…"

CHAPTER TWO

Cassie woke up even earlier than usual the next morning. The knowledge that Ellie was going to be coming in and inspecting the pizzeria for the first time since she had started working there made her anxious, even though she kept telling herself there was nothing to be worried about. She'd stayed late the night before, working a double shift, to make sure that everything was left as it should be when they closed for the night. It wasn't that she didn't trust her employees, but she didn't want to take any risks. She was determined to make sure everything was perfect when Ellie saw the place for the first time in months.

Getting up, she wandered into the kitchen, fed her cat, Sparrow, and started the coffee. Antonio had come over the evening before when she finally got out of work and had taken two of the three pizzas she and Bridget had left over. The last one was still in the fridge, and she cut herself a cold slice for breakfast. "Waste not, want not," she muttered as she poured herself some coffee, added cream and sugar, and then went to sit at the table.

The sound of the guest room door opening followed a moment later by the bathroom door closing and the water in the shower running made her double-check the time. Bridget was fond of sleeping late, sometimes even past noon, and Cassie was still getting used to her sister rising this early. Twice a week, Bridget had to be at work by seven o'clock for opening, but she didn't have to arrive until ten on the other three days. It was a minimum-wage job, but it was close to the apartment, and it was a small grocery store, not part of a national chain. Bridget seemed comfortable there and happy with her coworkers, which Cassie knew could make all the difference.

Her sister waking up so early was still going to take some getting used to.

"Good morning," Cassie said a little while later when her sister came out of the bathroom, her hair still soaking wet. Bridget made a zombielike noise and staggered over to the coffee pot, where she poured herself a steaming cup. She drank it black, a sight that made Cassie wince, then walked over to the couch and collapsed onto it.

"How do you do this every morning?" her sister groaned.

"You get used to it." Cassie shrugged, then grinned. "Also, I don't stay up until two thirty every morning."

"I'm just not tired earlier," Bridget complained. "I'm probably half vampire or something. I'm made for the nightlife."

"Unfortunately for you, both our parents are very human," Cassie said. "Thank you for doing the grocery shopping yesterday, by the way. If you give me the receipt, I'll send you my half of what it cost. You … did end up buying all that cheese, I noticed."

Her sister gave her a tired grin. "I wasn't joking. You really did use all of our cheese. Also, we were having a sale. I got some of that cheese at thirty percent off. It should last us a while, unless you go on another pizza-making spree."

"I go on a pizza-making spree every single day, just usually at the restaurant."

"True," her sister said. "You got me there. Hey, isn't this the day your boss is supposed to get here?"

"She flew in last night. She said she would probably stop in at the pizzeria today, though."

"Right. Maybe I'll stop in today after work. It would be neat to meet her."

"I'll send you a text once she's there, if you'd like," Cassie said, shrugging. "I don't know why you'd want to meet my boss, though."

"She seems nice," Bridget said. She hugged a pillow to herself, then yawned and checked her phone, frowning at the time. "I guess I'd better get ready to go. I'll see you this evening."

"Have a nice day at work," Cassie said as her sister got up and walked back toward the guest room.

Cassie took extra time getting ready that morning. It wasn't as if she usually dressed like a slob, but the fact that she would be seeing her boss in person for only the second time made her pay extra attention to what she wore, her makeup, and her hair. Only after checking herself in the mirror for the third time did she tell herself she was being ridiculous. There was no reason for her to be this worried about seeing her boss again. Everything would be all right. The pizzeria was in good shape, her customers were happy, and they had a popular, if not very out-of-the-box, special. Ellie would have nothing to be disappointed in. Cassie had been doing a good job, and she knew it.

She walked to the restaurant that morning instead

of jogging, not wanting to risk being out of breath if Ellie decided to come in early. When she arrived, she did one last check around the building to make sure everything was still perfect, then started on the morning routine, taking extra care to make sure each of the pizzas she prepared didn't have so much as a single slice of pepperoni out of place.

The morning went by slowly, and gradually, Cassie relaxed. She almost wasn't expecting it when, around two, the pizzeria's door opened and she looked up to see a familiar face, even if one she had mostly seen over video calls.

It took all of her willpower to do nothing but shoot Ellie a smile while she continued speaking with the customer she was ringing up. Once they had gone to a table to wait, she turned her full attention to her boss, who stepped up to the counter. There was an older woman with her, and it took Cassie a few seconds to recognize her as the woman in the pictures that were hanging on the pizzeria's wall. This was the famous Nonna, otherwise known as Ann Pacelli, the wife of the man who had opened the original Papa Pacelli's up in Kittiport. She lived near there in a retirement community, but according to Linda, Nonna didn't stop in at the pizzeria as much as she used to.

"Hey, Cassie," Ellie said with a smile. "The place

looks great. Do you think Nonna and I could get a couple slices of the Chicago-style deep dish?"

"Of course," Cassie said, hoping that Letha, who was on kitchen duty, had followed her instructions to a tee. The Chicago-style deep dish was a lot different than anything else they'd made, and it was taking her employees some time to get the hang of it.

She called back for the slices, got Ellie and Nonna their drinks, then went back to the kitchen to get their food. When she took it to the table, Ellie said, "If you haven't already eaten and want to grab yourself some lunch, it would be lovely if you would join us. Do you have someone who can cover the counter for you?"

"Yes. Just a second and I'll let Maddie know. She's been catching up with some of the dishes."

She went off to fetch her employee and a slice of pizza for herself, though she opted for one of the thin crust cheese pizzas that they sold by the slice, having had her fill of the deep dish. A minute later, she joined Ellie and Nonna at their table. Ellie introduced her to the older woman, and Cassie shook her hand, feeling like she was finally meeting a legend.

"How was your flight?" she asked Ellie after she greeted Nonna.

"It wasn't terrible," Ellie said. "It was a bit bumpy about midway through, but after that, things smoothed out. I've got to say, it's nice to be back in Florida. I won't be at the restaurant too much. I'm mostly just here to visit Nonna, but I do want to catch up with all of the employees here and take the time to talk with you, in case you have any questions. I know your training with Linda was a little bit rushed."

"Of course," Cassie said. "Just let me know when, and I'll make it work."

"Why don't you come over to the condo?" Nonna asked. "I can make dinner for everyone. I hardly get the chance to cook anymore."

"That would be lovely," Ellie said with a smile at her grandmother. "If you're comfortable with that, Cassie, we can tentatively plan to have a dinner at the condo later this week. And if there's anyone you'd like to bring, of course, they're welcome."

"Actually, would you mind if I asked my sister?" Cassie asked. "She's staying with me right now, and she said she wanted to meet you."

"Of course, I'd love to meet her," Ellie said. "Now, could you remind me of your employees' names? I know I have them on file, but it's hard to match the names with faces. That girl at the register, is that Sonja?"

Cassie shook her head. "That's Maddie. She's been here two years..." The rest of her impromptu

CHAPTER THREE

When she got back to the apartment that evening, she extended the invitation to dinner to Bridget, who was making cheese fondue on the stove. After asking Bridget about the dinner and getting an eager agreement to attend from her sister, Cassie couldn't help but ask about the fondue.

"Well, we have a lot of cheese," Bridget said. "And there was a bottle of wine that you opened last weekend that you weren't finishing, and you said you didn't want me drinking it since I'm under twenty-one, so I figured... Well, cheese and wine... All I needed to do was pick up some good bread from the bakery at the store. We haven't had fondue since my high school graduation dinner."

"Well, it looks good," Cassie said. "Do you want

me to make something else to go with it? We should probably have more than bread and cheese for dinner."

"I got a rotisserie chicken too," Bridget said. "Speaking of buying things, I left the receipt on the counter, if you want to pay me half."

"All right," Cassie said. "How are you liking work?"

"It's all right," Bridget said, turning back to the double boiler on the stove. "I mean, it's not something I want to do forever, but I guess it's nice to have a paycheck to look forward to. I'm almost out of the money I got from selling my textbooks and clothes."

"What do you think you're going to do long term?" Cassie asked. "Not to pressure you, but it would be nice to know if you have some sort of plan. Do you think you will go back to school?"

"I don't know." Her sister frowned at the fondue, stirring with more force than necessary. "I still don't know what I want to do, Cassie. Like, I feel like there should be something I'm passionate about, something I want to spend my life doing, but I can't figure out what it is. I guess if I find something that I'm passionate enough about, I'll go back to school for it."

"If you want, after Ellie leaves and things settle down at the pizzeria a bit, I'll help you go through different jobs you think you might be interested in, and we can probably figure out a way for you to job shadow some people in that industry. It would be a good way for you to learn if you're interested in the actual work."

"Yeah, that might help," her sister said. She shot Cassie a tight smile. "I really appreciate it, Cass, but could we not talk about it right now? I kind of just want to have a relaxing evening."

"All right," Cassie said. "I'll get changed, then I'll slice the chicken. You know what, I bet it would taste great dipped in the fondue."

The next morning, she left to meet Antonio for coffee before the bank opened. His hours were very regular, Monday through Friday from nine to six with a lunch break somewhere in the middle. If she had to be at the pizzeria earlier in the mornings, she would probably meet him for coffee almost every day, but as it was, she had to get there by eight thirty if she wanted to have any time to chat with him before he had to get to the bank. It was a bit too much time to wait around afterward until she had to be at work but not quite enough time to justify going back home and coming out again, so their morning meetings were reserved for the more important chats.

In this case, he wanted to hear all about Ellie since

she'd been talking about her boss's visit for a long time. He'd arrived before her and had ordered the daily special drink for her, knowing that she would want to try it. It had pink foam on top; she was already delighted. Once she sat down, she sipped it, the sweet, warm coffee seeming to energize her even before it hit her stomach. She leaned back in her chair and sighed. "You were right, and I was wrong."

"Oh?" he said, raising an eyebrow. "About what? I'm probably right about a lot of things."

She rolled her eyes at him, but paired it with a smile. "About Ellie, of course. She only had nice things to say. I was worrying for no reason."

"I told you," he said. "I mean, I may not spend all day every day at the pizzeria, but from what I've seen, you're a great boss. Your employees seem to like you, you haven't had any major complaints from your customers, and you make good food. Ellie is probably just glad that she has someone she can trust down here."

"She's so nice. She invited me and Bridget to dinner this week at her grandmother's house." Cassie felt a little bit guilty for not even thinking of inviting Antonio. She probably would have if it hadn't been for Bridget. But it might be a little bit strange to invite a guy she wasn't even dating to dinner with her boss.

"See? You've got nothing to worry about."

"I know, I know." She sighed, taking another sip of her coffee. "So, how have you been?"

He shrugged. "Oh, nothing new ever really happens in my life, so I don't have much to say about it. I go to work, wait around for something interesting to happen, which almost never does, then go home and repeat the process the next day."

"At least it's not a stressful way of life," Cassie said. "You know, I've been here in Miami for months now, and I haven't even spent a day at the beach yet. Do you want to go with me some weekend?"

"Of course," Antonio said, grinning. "That sounds like it'll be a lot of fun. Do you want to go this weekend?"

"Maybe," Cassie said. "I mean, I definitely want to, but Ellie will still be in town, and I don't want to commit to anything without knowing when she wants to have dinner, or if she wants to meet up for anything else. I'll let you know?"

He nodded and opened his mouth to reply but closed it again when her phone started to buzz in her purse. She took it out, checked the caller ID, and frowned. "Talking about her must've summoned her. It's Ellie. Do you mind if I answer it?"

He waved the question aside. "Of course not. Go ahead. I'm curious about what she wants too."

Cassie pressed the button to answer the call and raised the phone to her ear. "Hey, it's Cassie."

"Hi, Cassie. I'm so sorry to call you like this, and if you're too busy, it's no problem at all. My rental car somehow got damaged overnight, and the company won't be able to send a tow truck out until later today. They offered to give me a ride back to the agency so I can get a different car when the tow truck arrives, but I want to pick the new car up earlier than that. Is there any chance you could pick me up and take me to the rental car agency? It's only about twenty minutes from my grandmother's condo. Like I said, if you're busy, don't worry about it at all. I can call another ride."

Cassie hesitated. "Well, I don't have a car either, I've just been taking cabs when I need to—"

She broke off when Antonio tapped her arm to get her attention. "You can take the SUV" he said, keeping his voice low. "I don't mind. I won't need it until six."

She raised her eyebrows, and when he nodded, she grinned at him. "You know what, actually I do have access to a vehicle. Could you send me your grandmother's address? I can probably be there in about half an hour."

"Are you sure? I don't want to put you out."

"I'm sure. I really don't mind at all."

"Well, thanks, Cassie. I'll send you the address."

Cassie said her goodbyes and ended the call, then turned to Antonio. "Are you sure? I don't want to just leave you without a vehicle."

"I'll be at work all day. I really don't mind. I could only hear a little of what she said. Was she in an accident?"

"She didn't say. I guess I'll find out when I get there."

"Let's head over to the bank. I parked there. I'll give you the keys."

"Thanks. I'll fill it up for you before I bring it back."

"No need. If you feel like returning the favor, just keep me updated on what's going on. I'm kind of curious now."

She laughed, draining the rest of her coffee so she could dump the cup in the garbage on her way out. "I will. Trust me; I'm curious too. I'll give you the details as soon as I get a chance."

CHAPTER FOUR

It had been a while since Cassie had driven, and her own vehicle, before she'd sold it, had been a sedan. Being behind the wheel of Antonio's SUV was a different experience altogether. It was almost painful to navigate the busy streets of Miami with it, and she had to wonder why he didn't sell it for something a bit smaller and more fuel-efficient.

She shouldn't complain, though; she was still a little bit surprised that he had been comfortable lending her his vehicle in the first place. The fact that he trusted her with it, made her feel good. She took extra care as she followed the road out of town and toward the address Ellie had sent her.

The condo community was a few miles out of town and down the coast. As she drew nearer, Cassie saw more and more palm trees and white, sandy beaches. She didn't even want to think about how much it would cost to live in this area. She'd thought her own apartment building, which had a security guard and an elevator, was expensive. The condos must cost two or three times what she was paying each month.

She slowed as she drew near the complex, spotting the familiar flashing red and blue lights of police vehicles. For a moment, she wondered if Ellie had been in an accident after all, but there was no sign of a wrecked car anywhere. Instead, the police were standing off to the side of the road in the ditch. A couple of them were taking pictures of something, and there was an ambulance waiting nearby. Cassie made sure there was no oncoming traffic, then got over and eased past the emergency vehicles, trying hard to resist the temptation to stare. She wasn't entirely successful, and caught a glimpse of a pair of shoes in the ditch. A pair of shoes that were still attached to feet, which were attached to a person lying on the ground and not moving.

The sight filled her with a dull sickness, and she hurried past, turning into the condo entrance which was just beyond the scene of the accident. Shaken, she followed the GPS on her phone until she spotted her boss standing in front of one of the condos, talking to a few other people. There was a dark gray sedan pulled up along the curb with the corner of its bumper completely crushed in. The sight made Cassie raise her eyebrows. Ellie didn't strike her as a reckless driver, but that looked like the result of a pretty serious crash. She wondered what had happened as she pulled up to the curb in front of the sedan. The driveway looked like it had just been redone, and it was roped off from the street. Cassie got out of the SUV and approached the small group gathered on the perfectly manicured grass.

"Oh, hi, Cassie," Ellie said, turning around as Cassie approached. "You made it out here faster than I thought you would. You know Nonna, and this is Sheila, Nonna's neighbor. Evan is the groundskeeper here."

"It's nice to meet you," Cassie said to them. "I'm just here to help Ellie get to the rental car agency. That damage looks pretty bad."

"I know," Ellie said, frowning. "I have no idea how it happened. That's what we've been discussing."

"You just found it like this?" Cassie asked, turning back to look at the vehicle. "That's really odd."

"It had to have happened sometime during the

night," the groundskeeper, Evan, said. He was a middle-aged man with a graying beard and sweat stains on his worn-out T-shirt. There was a truck with a trailer that held a lawnmower parked a little ways down the street; she assumed it was his vehicle. "Like I said, I noticed it when I came in this morning. And I got here just after five."

"This place isn't exactly busy at night," Nonna said. "Half the residents don't even drive. It just doesn't make sense that someone would run into the car accidentally and not say anything. It had to have been on purpose."

Sheila, the other elderly woman, shook her head and tsked. "What a shame. Your insurance should cover that, though, right, Ellie? I'd hate for you to have to pay for that damage out of pocket."

"I'm sure there will be an investigation of some sort," Ellie said, frowning at the vehicle herself. "I have no idea how the damage happened, and there isn't a police report for the insurance company to look over, I don't know what the next steps will be."

"So, you could have to end up paying for it?" Sheila asked. "That's a nice vehicle. Repairs might be expensive."

"I hope I don't have to pay for it out of pocket," Ellie said. "But there's not much I can do either way."

"It's a relatively common model," Evan said, peering at the car. "They should be able to get parts for it easily, at least."

"Speaking of vehicles, when did you get a new truck, Evan?" Sheila peered at the shiny white truck that was parked down the road. "I thought you refused to part with that beater."

Evan gave a dry laugh. "Hey, we've all got to leave our comfort zone sometime, huh? I saw that beauty in the dealership's lot this morning, and knew it was time to say goodbye."

"You think the repairs won't be too expensive?" Ellie asked, bringing the conversation back to the damage to her car. "I've heard body damage like this can cost thousands. I just wish I knew who did this. What sort of person crashes into someone's car and doesn't even leave a note? Who would even be driving that recklessly in an area like this?"

"Do you think it has something to do with all the police that are gathered outside the complex?" Cassie asked, walking a bit closer to join the little group more completely as she got drawn into the conversation.

"The police?" Evan asked, raising one of his bushy eyebrows. "I don't know anything about that."

"There are police here?" Sheila asked. "I didn't

think they'd investigate something like this. Did someone call them?"

"No, they're outside the condo complex." She hesitated, then said, "I might be wrong, but it looks like there's a body out there, in the ditch along the road."

Nonna pressed a hand to her mouth, and Ellie's eyes widened. "That's horrible. What happened?"

"I have no idea," Cassie said. "I was hoping one of you would know."

"I wonder if it was that real estate lady," Evan said with a frown. "Her car was still parked at the clubhouse when I got here this morning. I figured I'd report it after lunch if it was still there."

"What was her name again? Riley?" Sheila asked.

"Ryanne," Nonna said, pursing her lips. "I don't know why she'd still be here, though. I hope nothing bad happened to her."

"One of us should go ask the police," Sheila said. "Ellie, dear, you said your husband is a sheriff, right? You should do it."

"I don't think the police would appreciate someone walking up to them and asking for details about what's going on, especially if they're in the middle of a homicide investigation," Ellie said. "We'll just have to wait and see what happens. Sorry this is taking so long, Cassie. Let me just run in and grab my purse, then we can get going."

"There's no hurry," Cassie said. "I'm not going to lie, I'm curious about all of this too. Who is this real estate lady you're talking about, and why would someone have killed her?"

"She's this horrible person who wants to buy up the community from the current shareholders," Sheila said, crossing her arms. Her permed gray hair bobbed whenever she moved her head. "She wants to expand into apartments and rebrand completely. Everyone got notices about it in their mailboxes a couple of days ago, and she was here yesterday poking around, asking questions, and taking pictures. No one liked her; we are all happy with the way things are now. Of course, I don't think anyone would've actually killed her over it, but she definitely had a lot of people unhappy with her."

"If it was her, I bet we'll hear about it in a day or two," Nonna said. "We'll just have to wait until then to see what's going on. Remember, Cassie said she wasn't even sure she saw a body."

"I mean, I'm like, ninety percent sure," Cassie said.

Everyone in their little group looked up at the sound of a vehicle coming around the corner. They fell silent, even though there was no way the person inside the car would have been able to hear them talking. Cassie couldn't help but give a quiet huff of laughter at how strange they must look to the person in the slightly beat-up coupe; she could just see it now, a mismatched group with two old ladies, two younger women, and a scruffy groundskeeper, all turning their heads simultaneously to look at the new arrival as she pulled up to the curb. As soon as the vehicle was parked, a woman stepped out of the driver's side door.

"Hold on, I recognize her," Nonna said. "We saw her yesterday at the clubhouse, Ellie. She's the one who got into a fight with the real estate developer and got kicked out. She was in a different car, though. That's odd."

"I wonder what she's doing back here?" Ellie said, frowning.

"If she was kicked out, she certainly shouldn't be coming back," Sheila said, crossing her arms. "Evan, go deal with her."

"I'm just here to cut the grass," Evan said. "I'm not security."

"Well, Ann and I can hardly kick her out ourselves," Sheila said. "And Ellie and Cassie are guests."

"It's not my job," Evan said, raising his hands. "I've got to get back to my actual work; I've had enough of all this gossiping. I'll keep my ears open and see if I can figure out what happened, but not all of us can sit around chatting with the neighbors all day. Your grass doesn't keep itself short."

With that, he walked back down the sidewalk to his truck. Sheila sighed and turned back to the car, which had stopped across the street from them. "Well, he's not exactly the most helpful fella, is he?"

"He is right," Nonna said fairly. "It isn't his job. It looks like she wants something, though. She looks nervous about approaching us. She must know she's not supposed to be here."

"I'm going to go talk to her," Sheila said. "We really don't need any more trouble today."

With that, the elderly woman stepped across the street, leaving Ellie, Nonna, and Cassie on their own. Ellie turned to Cassie and gave her a tight smile. "Well, welcome to the drama that is my life."

Nonna laughed. "You can't escape it even when you're my age. Things usually aren't this bad here, though. That real estate lady, Ryanne, got people talking, and everyone's wound up about that. Now with what happened to Ellie's car, and if you're right that there really was a death just outside the complex..."

Well, a lot of us don't have much better to do with our time than gossip."

"It's okay," Cassie said with a smile. "I really don't mind. My morning is turning out a lot more interesting than I expected it to be, that's for sure."

"I hope I didn't take you away from anything important," Ellie said. "We can get going, if you'd like."

"Take your time," Cassie said.

A scream cut through their conversation, and all three of them looked across the road to where Sheila had fallen to the ground. The woman who Sheila had gone to talk to had a horrified look on her face. Ellie started running across the road, and Cassie followed her, arriving just as the woman stepped forward to try to help Sheila up.

CHAPTER FIVE

"I'm so sorry," the woman kept saying. They had helped Sheila up, and the older woman was a bit bruised, but unhurt.

"You pushed me," she snapped. "I want you arrested! That was assault."

"No, no it wasn't," the woman said. "I didn't mean to push you! You just came up to me so fast, and I had no idea who you were, and ... and it was a reflex. I have a lot going on. These past few months have been horrible for me."

"I could've broken my hip! You aren't even supposed to be here."

"I thought someone here would know what's going on," the woman said. "Can we just start over? Please? My name is Verity Hendrick, and I'm so, so sorry for what happened. Can I talk to you for a minute, though? I'm trying to figure out what happened to Ryanne Dallas. She was killed last night, and I doubt I'll be able to get anything out of the police."

"You're talking about the real estate developer, right?" Ellie asked, stepping forward. Nonna gently guided Sheila back. The older woman was still fuming, but seemed curious too.

"Yes," Verity said. "Good, I'm glad you know who I'm talking about. She was hit by a car last night and died. The police are gathered right outside this condo complex. Have you heard anything about what happened?"

"We first heard about it five minutes ago," Ellie said. "It sounds like you know more than we do. How do you know what happened?"

Verity hesitated. "I … I can't tell you my sources. But I highly suspect it was a hit-and-run. I'm just… Look, I was suing her, all right? Now that she's dead, I'm not going to get anything at all. I just want to know what happened."

"Well, none of us know," Ellie said. She glanced back at Sheila, who was still holding her elbow and was now muttering to Nonna. "I think you should probably go. I do remember you getting asked to leave yesterday."

"Oh," Verity said. She hesitated, looked back at Sheila, then seemed to deflate a bit. "I'll go. I really am sorry. I didn't mean to shove her. I just… I need to think before I react."

She hesitated, as if waiting for one of them to tell her it was okay, but none of them said a word. After a moment, she got back into her car. She pulled away from the curb just as a tow truck came around the curve. It was followed by a police vehicle, which chirped at them, flashing its lights once before pulling over in front of Cassie's borrowed SUV. She met Ellie's eyes and raised an eyebrow.

"I guess they were able to get here earlier than expected," Ellie said. She grimaced. "I'm so sorry, Cassie. I just wasted so much of your time."

"It's fine. I'm more curious about what's going on than anything else.

"Trust me, so am I." They walked back across the street, and Ellie hung back to speak with her grand-mother quietly. When they reached the other side of the street, Nonna went into Sheila's house with her while Ellie turned to talk to the police officer who was approaching them along with the tow truck driver. Both of them stopped by Ellie's rental vehicle and examined the damage to the bumper. Cassie realized with a jolt what was going on.

A woman had been found, killed by a hit-and-run driver, right outside the condo complex. Ellie's vehicle had unexplained damage to the bumper. It had to look extremely bad to the police.

"Is this your car, ma'am?" the officer asked, turning to her. She took a step back, shaking her head, and Ellie stepped forward.

"I'm renting it. My name is Eleanora Pacelli. How can I help you?"

"A woman was struck and killed by a vehicle not far from here last night," the officer said. "Mind if I ask how this damage to your car happened?"

Cassie winced, watching Ellie's face pale. "I'm not sure how it happened, sir."

The officer frowned at her. "Did anyone else drive it yesterday?"

"No. My name is the only one on the rental agreement, and besides, I'm staying with my grandmother, and she can't drive."

"So, you are the only one who has driven this vehicle, but you don't know how the damage to it occurred?"

"I know how it sounds, but I really don't," Ellie

said. She sighed. "I know how it looks. What do you need from me?"

"I'm going to have to ask you to come in for questioning, ma'am," the officer said. "Will you get in the back of the squad car, please?"

"Can I get my purse first?" Ellie asked, biting her lip.

"Ma'am, please get in my squad car. I'll have to put you under arrest if you refuse."

"I'll go get your purse," Cassie said. "Where is it?"

"Just inside, on the end table by the door," Ellie said, allowing the police officer to escort her to the squad car.

Cassie nodded and jogged to Nonna's condo. She pushed open the door, stepped into the cool air-conditioning, and jumped back when a tiny Chihuahua yapped at her. She looked down at the little dog, then crouched to let it sniff her hand. "Hey there, sweetie. Sorry for scaring you. I've just got to grab something, and I'll be out of your hair."

After letting the dog sniff her for a few seconds, she stood up and looked around, spotting the purse right away. She grabbed it, and then left the condo, carefully closing the door behind her so the Chihuahua couldn't get out. She jogged over to where the officer was waiting and handed him the purse, then watched as he got into his vehicle and said something into his radio.

A moment later, he pulled away from the curb. Cassie's last sight of her boss was of Ellie looking at her through the window, her expression one of exasperation mixed with embarrassment. Cassie gave her a weak smile that she hoped was, somehow, reassuring, then looked around, not sure what to do. It seemed she wasn't giving Ellie a ride after all. Nonna was in the other condo and didn't know what had happened to her granddaughter. She should tell her before she left.

Before she could do anything, the tow truck driver approached her, jabbing his thumb back toward the SUV and Ellie's rental car. "That your SUV, miss?" he asked.

"Yes, it is, do you need me to move it?"

He nodded. "If you wouldn't mind, I'd appreciate it." He sighed, looking back toward where the police cruiser was just turning out of sight. "Gotta say, I feel a bit bad. That officer stopped me as I was turning into the complex and asked what was going on. I told him I was going to pick up a car that had some damage to the front bumper. He followed me in here. I guess I can see why, if he is really dealing with a hit-and-run. I hope I didn't just get someone innocent arrested, though."

"I'm sure she's innocent, but they'll figure it out," Cassie said. "I can understand how bad it looks. I'll go move the SUV."

She did so, parking the vehicle in Sheila's driveway before getting out. The tow truck driver waved to her in thanks, and she waved back, then walked up to Sheila's door, knocking twice on it.

Nonna was the one who opened it. "What is it, dear? Did Ellie need something?"

Cassie took a deep breath and shifted on her feet. "Ellie's been taken in for questioning. I just thought you should know."

CHAPTER SIX

Nonna was understandably upset when Cassie told her that her granddaughter had been taken into the police station in the scant few minutes she'd been out of sight. There was nothing she could do, though, just like there was nothing that Cassie could do.

She promised Nonna she'd help if Ellie needed a ride somewhere, asked her to keep her updated, then said her goodbyes, getting back behind the wheel of her SUV and pulling out of the condo complex. The ambulance had left, and most of the police vehicles were gone, but there were still two of them, and the area around the site of the accident was cordoned off with cones.

She inched her way around the accident and then

increased her speed as she drove back down the road, her mind racing.

It was impossible not to see how bad Ellie looked from an outside perspective. Major damage to a car didn't just happen without a reason, and if she was the detective in charge of the case, she wouldn't believe Ellie when she said she didn't know how it happened. But ... she just couldn't see her boss committing a hit-and-run. Was she too biased? Did she just want to think the best of the woman who had hired her? A small, selfish voice in the back of her mind wondered what would happen to the pizzeria–what would happen to her–if Ellie got convicted of a crime like this. She forced the thought away. There were more important things to worry about. A woman was dead, and a likely innocent woman had been taken in for questioning. There was nothing Cassie could do except wait, and that was something she had never been good at.

The day spent working at the pizzeria was full of awkward moments. The employees all knew that Ellie was coming to town, and everyone working that day wanted to hear about the boss. Cassie didn't want to tell them what had happened yet, but she also didn't want to lie, so she had to be vague with her answers, which got her some odd looks.

She remembered, belatedly, that Ellie's husband was a sheriff. Surely he'd be able to do something to get his wife out of lockup? He was probably the first person Nonna had called when Cassie left. The knowledge that Ellie had someone who knew how the law worked in her corner made Cassie feel better, and she felt even better when, around three, she got a text message from Ellie telling her that she was back at the condo and apologizing again for all the trouble. Cassie messaged her back, reassuring her it was okay, and then left it at that. She had questions, but none of them were things she wanted to ask over text messages.

While she didn't want to tell her employees about what had happened, she didn't have the same reservations about Antonio and Bridget. After work, she stopped by the bank to wait for Antonio to get out, then asked if he wanted to come back to the apartment for dinner.

"Sure," he said. "Are we getting pizza?"

"Definitely not," Cassie said with a laugh. "I've had way too much pizza lately. How does Thai sound?"

"Sounds good to me. That little place by the beach?"

"That's what I was thinking. They get the food

ready pretty quickly. If I order now, we should be able to just swing by and pick it up. Let me call Bridget and see what she wants."

Less than half an hour later, she, Antonio, and Bridget were seated around her kitchen table, unpacking their orders and serving the Thai food onto Cassie's dishes. Cassie waited until everyone had their plates loaded with food, then took a deep breath.

"So," she began. "The police took my boss in for questioning today…"

She told the story the best way that she could, trying not to exaggerate anything. Still, when she was done, both of her companions were staring at her with wide eyes.

"Your boss is a murderer?" Bridget said. "Holy crap, Cassie, you've got to quit."

"I'm not quitting, and she's not a murderer," Cassie said, putting her fork down.

"Well…" Antonio said, his tone reluctant. "I trust your judgment, of course, but even you've got to admit that the fact that she claims not to know how the damage happened to her car is suspicious. It's a bit too coincidental, don't you think? A woman is killed in a hit-and-run, and your boss has significant damage to her front bumper the next morning, but miraculously doesn't remember how it happened?"

"I know it's coincidental, but she didn't do it," Cassie said. "She's so nice. So responsible. You haven't met her—either of you."

"What do you really know about her?" Bridget asked. "I mean, this is only like, what, the second time you've ever seen her in person? I know you talk on the phone with her and stuff, but all you probably talk about is business. You don't know what she's like in real life."

"Come on, guys. She's my boss. She can't be a murderer."

"The fact that she's your boss doesn't mean she can't also be a murderer," Antonio said. "I'm not saying she is, but I've got to agree with Bridget on this one. It looks suspicious."

Cassie gave him a betrayed look and turned back to her noodles, poking at them with her fork. Maybe they had a point. Maybe she was too close to the situation to see the truth.

No matter what she told herself, though, her gut feeling was that Ellie was innocent.

She got a chance to talk to her boss about what had happened the next day when Ellie and Nonna came in shortly after the lunch rush. Cassie was in the back working on a few pizzas for a delivery order when they came into the kitchen as if they owned the place. Which, Cassie had to remind herself, Ellie did.

"Whenever I visit, it makes me want to update the kitchen at the Kittiport location," Ellie said with a sigh, looking around. Cassie perked up; she'd never been to the main location.

"Is it very different?" she asked as she slid a ham and pineapple pizza into the oven. She washed her hands while Ellie answered.

"In some ways, yes. When I first took over, almost everything in the restaurant was decades old. My grandfather was a very traditional man, and as long as something worked, he would refuse to replace it. If something broke and he could get it repaired, he'd do that, or it was even better if he could repair it himself. I had to replace some of the appliances and update the interior, but I tried to keep it much the same. Kittiport is very different from Miami, and the people there just don't like change. The pizzeria already had a good number of regulars, and if it changed too much, I would risk losing them. Plus, Papa Pacelli's was nowhere near as successful then as it is now. I would've had to dip into my personal savings to modernize it as much as I did with this place." She looked around at the kitchen, smiling. "But at its core, it's the same. I don't know how you managed it, since this location is so much busier and so much more modern than the one in Maine, but walking in here makes me feel at home."

Cassie smiled. "I'm glad. I'll have to visit Kittiport sometime. I'd really like to see the original location at least once."

"Any time you feel like flying up, just let me know." Ellie returned the smile. "You're always welcome. You could even stay with Russell and me if you wanted."

"You could have her manage the other pizzeria and you could move down here," Nonna suggested slyly. "You always say how much you like visiting Miami."

Ellie laughed. "There's no way I am ever going to convince Russell to leave Maine," she said. "Plus, I doubt Cassie wants to live somewhere so cold."

"I'm a warm weather sort of girl," she agreed, smiling.

"Cassie, listen, I wanted to apologize again for what happened yesterday," Ellie said, moving over to lean against the counter as the conversation took a turn for the serious. "They let me go after questioning me, but I understand that it probably looked very bad. I just wanted to assure you that if you aren't comfortable with the situation, I don't blame you at all, and

I'll stay out of your hair for the rest of my visit. I just hope you'll give me the benefit of the doubt."

Cassie sighed. "I'll be honest with you; I don't know what to think. From what I know of you, there is no way that you would have committed a hit-and-run. But I can also see why the police were concerned. I haven't told the employees anything yet; I don't plan on doing so until we have some solid answers. I believe that people are innocent until proven guilty, though. I don't want this to affect our working relationship, especially not when everything I know about you tells me you didn't do it."

Ellie smiled, looking relieved. "Thanks, Cassie. That means a lot to me. Would you and your sister still like to come over for dinner?"

"I'd like that, and I'm sure she would too," Cassie said. Bridget would probably be thrilled to get the chance to "investigate" a possible murder suspect. Maybe dinner with her sister and her boss wasn't such a good idea after all.

Something must have showed on her face, because Ellie added, "If you'd like to bring anyone else, that's fine too."

"The more the merrier," Nonna assured her. "I miss having big dinner parties."

"In that case, would it be all right if my friend

Antonio came along as well?" She had no doubt that he would want to join them, and while he shared Bridget's reluctance to believe in Ellie's innocence, at least he wouldn't be obvious about it.

"Of course. Does tomorrow night work?"

"It should," Cassie replied. "I'll check with the two of them and get back to you."

CHAPTER SEVEN

Ellie and Nonna stayed for a little while longer, Ellie helping out in the kitchen while Nonna stayed out front, chatting with customers. Once people realized who she was, most of them were thrilled to meet her. Her picture was hanging up in black-and-white on the pizzeria's wall, after all, and a lot of their regulars knew the pizzeria's story.

The other employees seemed happy to meet Ellie, if a little intimidated. Cassie let the other woman have some time to work one-on-one with them and get to know them while she bussed tables out front. It was late afternoon when Ellie and Nonna said their good-byes and Cassie walked them to the door.

"I'll let you know about tomorrow," she promised.

"I'm not sure what we will be having yet, but

we'll make something other than pizza," Ellie said with a wink. "This visit has been lovely, Cassie. You're doing a great job."

She watched Ellie and Nonna get into the new rental car and pull away from the curb, feeling much better about everything. No matter what Antonio and Bridget thought, there was no way Ellie had killed someone, accidentally or not.

She was just turning to go back inside when a vehicle that had been parked a little ways down the block pulled away from the curb just to park right in front of the restaurant. She didn't recognize the vehicle, but she recognized the woman who got out of it.

"Verity, right?" Cassie said, frowning at the woman as she drew near. She hadn't exactly made a good impression the day before.

"Good, you remember me," Verity said. She smiled at Cassie, but the expression was weak. She had dark circles under her eyes, and her hair was a mess. Cassie wasn't certain, but she thought she might be wearing the same clothes as she had been the day before.

"Can I help you?" They were still standing just outside of the pizzeria. Even though she didn't have a good reason to deny her entry, she wasn't sure she wanted this woman to come inside.

"Maybe. What did she want? That woman... Ellie?"

Cassie blinked at her. "Why?"

Verity looked around, as if checking to make sure no one was listening in, then leaned forward and said, "I think she killed Ryanne Dallas. I'm trying to get proof. Please, I need your help."

Cassie took a step back from the woman out of reflex. She smelled bad, as if she hadn't washed in days. "I'm sorry, but you have the wrong person. Ellie didn't do anything."

"You don't know that," Verity said, taking another step closer to Cassie. "You saw her car. And—and she had motive. She got in an argument with Ryanne the day before her body was found!"

"Miss, please stop," Cassie said, backing up until her back was against the restaurant's outer wall. She didn't know what to do. She didn't want to cause a scene, but this woman was unbalanced. "Why are you even involved in this? And how did you know that Ryanne's death was from a hit-and-run?"

Verity's eyes widened. She hesitated, then said, "I saw her, afterwards. In the ditch. I should have called the police, I know, but she was already dead, and she didn't deserve that dignity." She took a deep breath.

"But I think one of the residents saw me driving away, and now I need to prove I didn't do it."

"You just left her by the side of the road?" Cassie was horrified.

"She wrecked my life!"

"How?" Cassie asked, befuddled.

Verity took another deep breath. She seemed to notice that she was making Cassie uncomfortable and took a step back. "She bullied me into selling my home for a lot less than it was worth. I was going through a divorce at the time, and she convinced me that I had to sell the house then or the price was going to drop drastically. She acted like she was doing me a favor, buying it at the price she offered. I should have done more research, and I know I shouldn't have listened to her, but what she did was unethical. I lost tens of thousands of dollars thanks to her. I've been following her, trying to get proof that she practices shady business dealings. I have a lawsuit against her, but now I won't get anything, all because someone killed her before our court date. And now the lawyer I was working with thinks I did it! He's told me he's going to be forwarding some of our correspondence to the police. It's only a matter of time before they come after me. Please, I need your help. I know Ellie did this, and if I can just prove it, I'll at least be able to stay out of jail."

"I'm sorry," Cassie said, meaning it. "What happened to you sounds very unfair, but you have the wrong person. Ellie's my boss—and my friend. And I know she's innocent. There's nothing I can do."

Verity's lips trembled, and she stared at Cassie for a long moment. She looked on the verge of breaking down, but instead she just gave a single, sharp nod, and retreated to her car. Feeling bad, Cassie watched her pull away.

While her conversation with Verity put a damper on her day, she perked up a little bit after she got home from work and was able to talk to first Bridget, then Antonio, and both of them confirmed that they would be able to make it to Ellie's dinner the next day. She sent a quick text off to her boss, then spent the evening trying to relax and forget about how stressful the week had been so far.

CHAPTER EIGHT

The next day, she hurried home after work to change into a nicer outfit, then went down with Bridget to wait for Antonio. He was picking them up, since otherwise they would have to call for a ride. Sometimes not having a car was inconvenient, but Cassie felt that she didn't need one enough for it to be worth buying one. Plus, she'd have to pay for parking, and the lot was nearly a block away, and in the opposite direction of the pizzeria. It made more sense to live with the occasional inconvenience than it did for her to pay a ridiculous amount of money for a vehicle she might use once a week or less.

When the SUV pulled up outside the apartment building, Cassie nodded to the security guard and went out with Bridget to get inside. Antonio cleaned up nicely, and she shot him a grin as she buckled in.

"I like what you did with your hair."

He touched his gelled hair self-consciously. "You do? I wasn't sure about it."

She nodded. "It looks good."

"So does yours," he said with a smile. "Well, it always does."

Cassie felt Bridget kick the back of her seat, and she flushed, knowing that if she turned to look at her sister one or both of them would break out into giggles. She really needed to go out alone with Antonio more. Going places with her nineteen-year-old little sister in tow really put a damper on her style.

Antonio drove them out of the city and down the coast, letting out a low whistle when he saw the retirement community. "This is nice."

He eased the vehicle into the complex and followed Cassie's directions. Someone—probably Evan, the groundskeeper—was carefully edging the sidewalk across the road, and the cones had been removed from the end of Nonna's driveway, leaving an expanse of freshly laid concrete for them to park on.

The three of them got out of the SUV and made their way to Nonna's front door. It opened before any of them could knock on it, and Ellie welcomed them in. The air-conditioning was cranked up inside, and Cassie wondered if Nonna liked it so cold because she was used to living in Maine.

The same Chihuahua Cassie had seen before greeted them with a bark, and as Antonio shut the door behind them, Ellie smiled and bent down to pick her up.

"This is Amie," she said. "My grandmother rescued her from a shelter a few years ago. She's a sweetheart, but she likes to pretend she's a watchdog."

"She's adorable," Cassie said, smiling as Bridget cooed over the little dog. "She's smaller than my cat."

Ellie put the dog down and welcomed them further in, leading them toward the kitchen. "I didn't know you had a cat. What's her name? Or his?"

"Her name is Sparrow," Cassie said, pulling a picture up on her phone. She was always glad to show her pretty little tortoiseshell off.

Once they reached the kitchen, where Nonna was pouring them glasses of lemonade, they went around and introduced themselves. Nonna and Ellie had made eggplant parmesan with homemade garlic bread, and the scent of the meal was mouthwatering. Cassie was relieved that Bridget seemed more focused on the food than on asking Ellie pointed questions; she was still worried that her sister might entertain notions of being a private investigator one day, and Bridget wasn't exactly the most subtle person in the world.

"This is lovely," Nonna said a few minutes into the meal. "Thank you all for coming over. I don't get a chance to host guests often enough."

"Thank you for having us," Antonio replied. "This community seems lovely. How long have you lived here?"

"I've been here full time for less than a year, but I've been coming here during the winters for a few years. It really is a nice community. I miss Maine sometimes, but I fly up to see Ellie and Russell at least once a year. Having nice weather year-round has been a godsend, and I'm working on convincing some of my friends from back home to join me."

"You've been making plenty of friends here, though," Ellie said with a fond smile. "I'm surprised Sheila didn't want to come tonight. The two of you seem close."

"I'm surprised too," Nonna admitted. "That woman is a social butterfly. I hope she's feeling well; she's been keeping to herself for the past few days. She normally gives me rides to the store, but I think something might have happened to her car. I haven't seen it parked in the driveway lately."

"I'm sure everything is fine. She's probably just keeping to herself because I'm visiting," Ellie said. "I bet she doesn't want to feel like she's taking time away from you seeing your granddaughter."

Someone's foot collided with Cassie's ankle, and she looked around to meet Bridget's eyes. Her sister was giving her a pointed look, then over at Ellie. Cassie raised an eyebrow and gave a minute shrug. She had no idea what her sister was trying to tell her. Bridget sighed and pulled out her phone, holding it under the table to text on it. A moment later, Cassie's own phone buzzed from where she had shoved it in her pocket, but she pointedly ignored it. She wasn't about to start texting during a dinner with her boss.

When Bridget caught on that Cassie was ignoring her on purpose, she heaved a sigh and turned her attention back to the food. The meal was amazing; all of them had been eating with gusto. Antonio had finished his plate already, which Nonna noticed. She offered to get him more food and began getting out of her seat, but he quickly waved her down and took his own plate back to the counter to get himself a second serving. Cassie smiled, watching him as he did so. This time, when Bridget kicked her ankle, her sister had a smug, knowing look on her face. Cassie ignored it with a sniff and turned back to Ellie.

"Thanks again for inviting us over. This food is amazing. Would you mind if I asked for a recipe?"

"Of course not," Ellie said. "You know what, I'll send you a copy of my entire recipe book. My grandfather came up with a lot of them; he is the same one who came up with the recipe for the pizza crust. He was a genius in the kitchen, and all of his recipes are to die for. If you feel like adapting any of them for the pizzeria, go right ahead."

"I bet an eggplant parm pizza would be pretty good," Cassie mused. "I have to admit, coming up with the weekly specials has been a lot more difficult than I thought it would be. How have you done it every week for years? Don't you run out of ideas?"

"You can recycle them occasionally," Ellie said. "If I don't have inspiration for a particular week, sometimes I'll look back over what our most popular specials were from a few years ago and run one of them again. Or I'll take a previous special and make a few tweaks to it and run it as something new. As long as you don't have anything too similar from week to week, people won't care. And sometimes old favorites are even more popular than new specials. Oh, I've been meaning to tell you, if you ever notice that a specific special is doing extremely well, you can look into adding it to the main menu. As long as you're able to get all the ingredients from our suppliers, it shouldn't be an issue. I've been thinking of implementing a seasonal menu at the Maine location, so if you wanted to have a few of the more popular pizzas on rotation, that's something we could think about doing down here as well."

The conversation for the rest of the meal centered around work. It was nice to finally be able to ask some of the questions Cassie had had but hadn't felt were worth calling Ellie over, and she got some advice from the other women that would help her in the future. Time passed quickly, and before she knew it, Antonio and Bridget had begun clearing their plates. Bridget excused herself to go use the restroom while Nonna got up to begin the washing. Cassie was quick to excuse herself as well, not wanting the older woman to take on the work by herself. She managed to glance at her phone and saw that Bridget's message read, *If it wasn't your boss, maybe it was that Sheila lady. MISSING CAR??*

Her sister was reaching, but at least she had the good sense not to actually say anything. Cassie put her phone away and was just about to start scrubbing the plates in the sink when Bridget came wandering back into the kitchen, frowning.

"There's some weird guy walking around your yard," she said, directing her words to Nonna. "Is he supposed to be there? I saw him through the bathroom window."

Nonna frowned, and Ellie raised an eyebrow. After asking Bridget which direction he'd been going in, they all headed into Nonna's bedroom, which had a window that looked out into the side yard. Sure enough, a man was walking around with a measuring tape and his phone out, as if he was taking pictures. Cassie recognized him as the groundskeeper just as Ellie said, "Oh, that's just Evan. My grandmother introduced me to him a few days ago. He's the groundskeeper here."

"I wonder what he's doing, though," Nonna said, frowning. "I'm going to go ask him."

They all ended up going outside, the camaraderie and sense of curiosity making them stick together. Nonna was the one who approached Evan, who by then was crouched down next to her house and was measuring the distance between the drainage spout and the side wall. He looked up when they came around the corner, standing up as they approached him.

"Good evening, ma'am," he said, nodding at Nonna.

"Good evening, Evan. We were just wondering what you're doing. It looks like your measuring for something, but I haven't gotten any notices from the board about new installations."

"Well, we've been meaning to install some decorative rock gardens around the drainage areas for a while," he said. "You should've got a notice about it a few months ago. I just haven't had time to get around to it until now. As a matter of fact, I'm planning on getting around to all of those planned upgrades. And if there's anything specific you want me to do while I'm at it, just let me know. I'll have to check with the board if it's anything major, but I should be able to do the small things on my own time."

Nonna raised her eyebrows. "That's mighty industrious of you. Last time we talked, you were saying you didn't have time to do everything they wanted you to do, and were waiting until they hired another person to help you out."

He grinned at them. "Well, I guess I found the time. Is there anything else you want me to look into while I'm here?"

"Not that I can think of," Nonna said. "We'll let you get back to work. I'll have to check through the notifications from the past few months to refresh myself on what all you will be doing."

He nodded to them, retracted his tape measure, and headed over to the next house. Cassie watched him go, her eyes automatically drawn to the window that was facing them. She jolted when she saw a woman standing silhouetted in the window, watching them. She hadn't realized anyone was there.

Ellie must have seen her reaction because she followed Cassie's gaze. "Sheila?" she asked, sounding surprised.

Before she could say anything else, the woman flicked the curtains shut and vanished from their view.

CHAPTER NINE

"Ugh, I never knew I could be so full."

Cassie looked down at her sister, who was sprawled on the floor in front of the coffee table. They were back in Cassie's apartment, Antonio having dropped them off a few minutes earlier, but neither of them felt like doing much but sit there and watch TV. After they had gone back inside, Nonna had brought out a platter of brownies, and then insisted that they take leftovers from the meal home. Cassie had a Tupperware container full of eggplant parmesan in her fridge, and even though her stomach was full to bursting, she was already looking forward to eating it for her next meal.

"There is a reason their family has such a

successful restaurant business," Cassie said. "And I think we found that reason out tonight."

"Seriously," Bridget said. "I thought you were a good cook until I tried their food."

"Hey!"

Her sister grinned at her, then her expression sobered. "Something weird is definitely going on, though."

"What are you talking about?" Cassie asked, racking her mind for anything strange Ellie might have done that evening. As far as she was concerned, her boss had acted like a perfectly normal, innocent, non-murderous person.

"Um, that creepy old woman who was watching us? And that overly helpful groundskeeper guy? It's like something out of one of those horror movies where someone moves to a new neighborhood and everyone's all weird and then it turns out they're part of a cult or something."

"I mean, it's a retirement community. I doubt Sheila has much to do other than spy on the neighbors. She was probably just wondering what Evan was doing, the same way we were. We all gathered to look out a bedroom window as well, remember? That probably would have looked weird to anyone looking."

"Well, yeah, but why did she just close the curtains when she saw us looking at her? That's weird, Cassie. A normal person would at least wave or something."

"I have no idea," Cassie said with a sigh. "Are you telling me you think she's the murderer now too?"

"You heard them say that Sheila gives Nonna rides to the store," Bridget said. "If she can drive, then where's her car?"

"Probably in the garage," Cassie replied dryly. "Why would she have killed Ryanne? She doesn't have any more motive than Ellie does. Do you at least think Ellie's innocent now?"

Bridget shrugged. "As far as I'm concerned, they're both suspects. And they have the same motive, obviously. That real estate lady wanted to buy the retirement community and make a bunch of changes no one liked. Sheila lives there; she would have wanted to stop that. And Ellie's grandmother lives there and loves the place; Ellie would've wanted to stop it on her grandmother's behalf. Frankly, anyone who lives in that community might have done it. Even that groundskeeper guy—they're always the guilty ones in horror movies."

"Or, and hear me out, I know this is going to

sound like a crazy idea, but maybe Ryanne was just taking some pictures outside the retirement community when a drunk or distracted driver came along and hit her. It doesn't have to be some big conspiracy. Sometimes things just happen."

"You really think there's nothing at all suspicious about the creepy old woman spying on us? Or about the fact that your boss's car happened to be damaged in exactly the same way one might expect a vehicle to be damaged if they had hit a person? Come on, Cassie, you have no sense of adventure."

"It's not about a sense of adventure," Cassie said. "It's about not letting my imagination get me into trouble. I almost get the feeling you want her to be guilty."

"Of course, I don't," Bridget said. "I'm just worried about you." Her sister groaned and sat up, leaning against the coffee table. "You are too trusting."

Cassie sighed. "Look, I promise not to go into any dark alleys with Ellie, okay? It's not like I was going to, anyway."

"Or Sheila."

"I promise not to go into any dark alleys with Ellie's grandmother's eighty-year-old neighbor," she replied dryly.

"Come on, she's the perfect suspect," Bridget said. "She's old. She has nothing to lose. Even if she gets caught, they can't do anything but put her in prison for however long she has left. She will always know that she got arrested for what she viewed as a good cause, protecting the community she's come to love."

Cassie threw a pillow at her sister. "Go write a script for the thriller you are obviously thinking up, and quit accusing real people of horrible things."

Bridget laughed, claiming the pillow to put under her knees, and said, "Can you at least promise me you'll keep your eyes open if you go back there for whatever reason? At least try to look at stuff without those rose-tinted glasses of yours on?"

"I think you're the one who's wearing paranoia-tinted glasses," Cassie said. "But all right. I'll think on it, okay? I promise."

Her phone buzzed, and reading the text message that Anthony had just sent her was a good excuse to end the conversation. She raised an eyebrow when she saw the contents. *Want to go bowling tomorrow night? Some of my friends are going, and I'd love to introduce you to them.*

She grinned and texted him back, *Of course. I'd love to.*

"What are you smiling about?" her sister asked suspiciously.

Cassie wondered if Bridget realized just how much like their mother she sounded in that instant. Why did her nineteen-year-old sister have the ability to make her feel like a fifteen-year-old who had her first crush and was trying to hide that fact from over-bearing parents? Frankly, it was ridiculous. She couldn't wait until Bridget met someone she liked and she could get revenge. It would be glorious.

CHAPTER TEN

It had been ages since Cassie had gone bowling. She'd probably been in her early twenties; she knew she'd gone sometime between her junior and senior year of college. In the decades since, bowling alleys hadn't changed at all. She looked around and laughed as she and Antonio walked into the building.

"I feel like I just stepped back into the nineties."

"If you'd rather go somewhere else, we can," Antonio said. "My friends probably won't care too much if we ditch them."

"No, this will be fun." She wiggled her fingers. "I've just got to limber up."

Someone called out to Antonio, and he raised his hand in a wave, leading her over to one of the lanes where four other people were waiting. Cassie eyed them; there were two men and two women. Were they two couples? Was this a date? She wouldn't object, but she wished she knew for sure. Bridget would never let her live it down if she'd gone on a date with Antonio and hadn't even realized it.

"Hey, guys," Antonio said. "This is Cassie. Cassie, this is Tom, Katy, Omar, and Allison."

There was a chorus of, "Hi," and "How are you doing?" before they went up to the counter for their bowling shoes and to order refreshments and pizza. When the food came out, Antonio laughed at the look on Cassie's face.

"Yeah, I forgot to warn you. This place has terrible pizza."

"Is it even pizza?" she asked, prodding it. "I have my doubts."

"You run a pizza place, right?" Katy asked, taking a slice for herself. Cassie nodded. "I don't think I've ever been there. What's it called again?"

"Papa Pacelli's," she replied. "It's a small restaurant, with only two locations. The owner lives in Maine, but her grandmother moved down here, and she visited often enough that she decided to open a second location in Miami."

"They've got the best pizza I've ever had," Antonio said. "You guys should try it sometime."

"Aha, so you *don't* just go there to see Cassie," Omar said, grinning at them. "Good to know. I don't remember the last time I had actual, good pizza. We'll have to eat there soon."

"Hey, Katy, you're up," Allison said, coming back from the lane. Cassie gingerly took a slice of pizza, watching as the others bowled, then getting up for her own turn. It had been a while, but at least she didn't send the ball into the gutter, which she counted as a plus.

"Not bad," Antonio said when she came back. "You got a split."

"We should have done this while Nikki was visiting," Cassie said. "She's surprisingly good at bowling."

The night continued pleasantly as Cassie got to know Antonio's friends. They were indeed two couples, but they'd all known each other for years. Even though she was a newcomer, she felt right at home with them, and even managed not to get too flustered at their jokes and insinuations about how much Antonio talked about her. In truth, she was touched by how much he seemed to have told them about her, and it made her feel better; it was another indication that he returned the not-quite-platonic feelings she had for him.

After bowling, she and Antonio left the group to get some late-night coffee. Maybe she shouldn't be having caffeine this late, but getting coffee with Antonio was practically a tradition by now. There was a place they hadn't tried yet just a couple of blocks from the bowling alley. It closed in just five minutes, so they went through the drive-through, grabbed their cups, then went to park somewhere quiet to sip their drinks. Part of Cassie wanted to invite Antonio up to her apartment, just to hang out for a while longer and maybe watch some TV, but it would feel strange doing that with Bridget there. She wasn't exactly in a hurry for her sister to move out, but it would definitely be nice to have the place to herself again.

"Did you have a nice time?" Antonio asked.

"I did," she replied with a grin. "Thanks for inviting me. We should do that again sometime."

"Definitely. How are things going at work? Is your boss still around?"

"She is," Cassie admitted. "Bridget still thinks that she might have killed that woman. She also thinks my boss's grandmother's neighbor might have done it, so I would take her opinion with a grain of salt."

"You really don't think that any of them had anything to do with that real estate developer's death?" he asked. "I know you're probably sick of talking about it, but I'm honestly curious."

Cassie frowned, turning her warm cup of coffee around carefully in her hands. "I don't know. I really don't think *Ellie* did it, that's for sure. I know it doesn't seem like I know her that well, but even though I've only met her a few times in person, I've talked with her on the phone, over email, and over video chat a lot. I know the kind of person she is, and she would never have done something like that on purpose. Even if it was an accident—if she was distracted for a moment or the woman stepped out into the road unexpectedly—she wouldn't try to hide it. She's married to a sheriff, for goodness' sake. She's not a criminal. As far as whether anyone else we've met did it, I don't know. Maybe that weird lady, Verity, who's been stalking Ellie. Bridget wants me to poke around and try to find the truth out, but I don't know if I should. What would Ellie think if she realized what I was doing?"

Antonio took another sip of his coffee, a thoughtful expression on his face. When he was done, he said, "I guess the way I see it is that *someone* hit and killed that poor woman with their car. Whoever it was either did it on purpose, which is murder, or did it accidentally but tried to hide the fact and never called for help. They just left her there and drove off. For all we know, she might have survived if an ambulance came right away. If you can somehow bring her justice, shouldn't you? I know the police are looking into the case, but they can't be everywhere at once, and people tend to clam up around them. I'm not saying you should turn into a spy from some action flick or something, but I don't think it would be wrong of you to ask some pointed questions or maybe look around a little bit more than you normally would if you go back there."

"I probably would, if I went back there. But I don't see that happening. Ellie's got another rental car, so she doesn't need me to give her a ride, and she's only going to be here for a few more days. I doubt she'll invite us over for dinner again. She probably wants to spend the remaining time with her grandmother." She sighed. "It's not that I'm not curious, you know, but what am I going to do? Break into Sheila's garage and try to see if her car has a dent in it? Hire a private investigator to find out if Verity is a wanted criminal?"

Antonio sent her a grin. "Why not? The first one, at least. I feel like hiring a PI would be expensive."

She blinked. "What?"

"You don't have to actually break anything, but

why not go there, peek in through some windows, maybe see if the garage door is unlocked? I guess it's technically trespassing, but it's not as if you're going to steal anything or cause any damages. Won't it always bother you if you're left wondering? I have to admit, the way that old lady was staring at us through her window made me uncomfortable too. If she's acting suspicious, there might be a reason for it."

"Antonio!" she said. "I can't break into an old woman's garage."

"Just look through the windows, then. I'll go with you."

She hesitated, but everything Bridget had said—and all of the strange occurrences surrounding Ryanne Dallas' death—gnawed at her despite her protests. With a sigh, she set her coffee down in the cup holder. "Fine, but no breaking and entering. We'll just look in the windows, and see what we can see. And we are never—*never*—telling Bridget about this. I don't want her to get any ideas."

CHAPTER ELEVEN

Since Bridget knew about Cassie's maybe-date and would probably be waiting up to hear about it, Antonio dropped her back off at the apartment with a promise to come and pick her up again a few hours later for their, as he put it, clandestine operation. Cassie felt a thrill at the thought of what they were going to do, even though it still didn't sit completely right with her.

As she expected, Bridget was waiting for her. Her younger sister was sitting on the couch in the dark and reached up to dramatically flick on the lights when Cassie walked into the apartment.

"Well, well, well," Bridget said. "What are you doing home so late, missy?"

Cassie glanced at her phone, checking the time. "Bridget, it's not even ten o'clock yet."

"Don't wreck my fun. How was it? Did he kiss you? Did you win?"

"At kissing?"

"At bowling," Bridget said, rolling her eyes. "Wait, *was* there kissing?"

"No kissing, and I came in kind of in the middle at bowling." Cassie paused to lock the door behind her and take off her shoes. "It was a lot of fun, though. I'm glad I went."

"You two move so slowly," her sister said. "It's obvious you both like each other. I don't understand what you're waiting for."

"We've both got other stuff happening in our lives," Cassie said, going to sit on the couch next to her sister. "It will happen when—if—it happens. For now, I'm just happy to spend some time getting to know him better. It's not that I don't want a relationship right now, but I'm not in a hurry for it either."

"Oh, it'll happen," Bridget said. "I can't believe you came in somewhere in the middle at bowling, though."

"Really? I've never been great at it."

"I know," her sister said with a grin. "I'm just surprised you didn't come in dead last."

Cassie tossed a throw pillow at her sister's head and grabbed the TV remote while she was distracted, turning the television on. Antonio was supposed to pick her up again in three hours. She would just have to hope Bridget retired to her room before then.

Thankfully, Bridget went into her bedroom at midnight. Cassie was beginning to worry that it would be one of the nights where Bridget wanted to stay up until the early hours of the morning watching television, but she had an early day at the grocery store the next morning which meant a relatively early bedtime. Cassie turned off the TV and made a production of running the water in the bathroom and then shutting her bedroom door loudly, pretending that she'd gone to bed as well. She waited in silence for a few minutes, listening to the sound of her sister shifting on the bed in the other room, then eased her door open and tiptoed down the hall, silently thankful that she'd chosen an apartment that was new enough that the floors didn't creak when she walked.

She made sure she had her purse and her phone, then grabbed her tennis shoes from beside the door and slipped out of the apartment, doing her best to lock the door as quietly as possible behind her. Then she leaned against the wall and put her tennis shoes on, tying them quickly before hurrying over to the elevator. She was on her way down when Antonio texted her that he was there.

There was something exhilarating about sneaking out of the apartment in the middle of the night. Of course, it was a bit ridiculous that she, a nearly 30-year-old woman, had to sneak out of her own apartment, but that didn't do anything to dampen the thrill. She was still a bit worried that they were doing something illegal, but she was determined not to let it go any further than peeking in the garage windows. At the absolute worst, they were trespassing in someone's yard, and she wasn't even sure if that was a crime. People walked on other people's yards all the time, didn't they? It wasn't as if they were planning to break in or steal anything.

"Go, go, go," she said as she climbed into the front seat of Antonio's SUV. He took off from the curb as she shut the door and looked over at her, wide-eyed.

"Is Bridget following you or something?"

She grinned as she buckled her seatbelt.

"No, I'm just getting into this. I feel like a spy. Do you remember the way?"

"Yeah, it's a pretty straight shot down the coast." He grinned over at her. "Come on, admit it. This is kind of fun."

"I just really hope Ellie doesn't find out about it somehow. I'd be mortified."

Antonio slowed as they approached the retirement community twenty minutes later. When Cassie asked him what was wrong, he said, "I'm not sure if I should turn in or park along the road outside the entrance."

"When we were talking to the groundskeeper, he mentioned a clubhouse. Maybe you could park there? It would probably be less suspicious than parking in front of someone's house at random."

"Good idea. We'll have to drive around until we find it."

Thankfully, it wasn't that difficult to find. It was along the main road inside the condo complex, and there were signs pointing the way. The clubhouse was clearly marked, and the parking lot was empty except for the groundskeeper's truck. Antonio pulled into a spot that had a clear shot to the exit in case they needed to make a fast getaway, and both of them got out of the SUV. He paused long enough to lock it, and glanced back at the vehicle.

"I guess we could have tried to find a less suspicious-looking ride," he said.

"It's only a problem if someone notices it," Cassie said quietly. She looked around. The only lights on were the streetlights. Every single condo had dark windows. "Something's telling me there aren't very many night owls around here."

"Do you remember how to get to the right street from here? The woman we're after lives right next to your boss's grandmother, right?"

"Don't say it like that. It sounds like we're going to kidnap her or murder her or something," Cassie said. "But yeah, I think it's this way." She gestured, and they began walking on the sidewalk. She felt exposed under the streetlights, but there was no sign that anyone was awake to see them. Besides, walking down the sidewalk was hardly illegal. A bit suspicious at this time of night and in this area, maybe, but not illegal.

Before long, they came to Ellie's grandmother's street. They turned down it, keeping to the other side of the road for now. They were nearly across from Nonna's condo when she slowed, frowning. There was a car parked across the street from the condo. At first, she'd thought it was empty and hadn't paid it any mind, but she was pretty sure she'd just seen movement inside it.

"What is it?" Antonio whispered, leaning close to her ear.

"I think someone's in that car," she said quietly. "What if it's the police? What if they're watching the condo because of the investigation? Oh, my goodness, we should never have come here. We're going to be arrested."

"We're not doing anything wrong," Antonio whispered back. "Let's just walk by and see who it is."

Cassie bit her lip, and Antonio nudged her, holding out his hand. She took it, and he squeezed her fingers before they began moving again. She knew she was being ridiculous, but the thought of getting confronted by the police right outside of the condo her boss was staying in during the middle of the night made her feel sick with dread.

As they drew even with the car, she turned her head to look in through the driver's side window and locked eyes with the woman inside. She froze in instant recognition.

Verity. She was parked across the street from the condo Ellie was staying in, blatantly spying on the place.

"Who is that?" Antonio asked. She remembered that he hadn't been there either time that she'd had a run-in with Verity.

"It's a long story, but the easiest way to explain it is that she is a stalker. She was following the woman who died, and now she's following Ellie."

That was all she had time for because Verity

opened the driver's side door and got out of her car. She was careful to close it quietly before walking over to Cassie and Antonio.

"What are you doing here?" she hissed.

"I could ask you the same thing," Cassie whispered back. "I thought you were banned from this complex."

"I'm trying to solve a murder," Verity whispered back. "I'm not doing anything wrong."

"You're stalking an innocent woman," Cassie hissed. "I don't know what you think you're going to prove by watching her house in the middle of the night, but you should leave. You're not supposed to be here."

"What are you going to do about it?" Verity asked, her gaze cold. "I have just as much right to be here as you do."

"I haven't been banned," Cassie said. "And I'm not going to leave knowing that you're here watching the place where my boss is staying. If I have to, I'll call the police."

Verity hesitated, and for a moment, Cassie felt bad for her. The other woman looked worse than the last time she'd seen her. She was in a different car than before, and Cassie wondered where she kept getting them. She supposed it made sense that Verity would have to keep finding different vehicles if she wasn't welcome in the retirement community and wanted to hide her presence here.

"Fine," Verity said at last, her voice cracking. "I should have expected this. I should've known that no one would be on my side."

With that, she walked back over to her car, slamming the door as she got into the driver's seat. Cassie and Antonio both winced at the sound. The engine came to life, and the vehicle peeled away from the curb, shattering the silence of the night.

CHAPTER TWELVE

"We'd better hurry," Antonio said. "People will have heard that."

For a moment, Cassie considered suggesting they just go back to the SUV and forget the whole thing, but Sheila's condo was right there. Right across the street. None of the lights in the surrounding houses had come on yet. She realized she was still pulling his hand, so she squeezed it and began to run across the road, Antonio next to her. They slowed as they reached the sidewalk and then the grass on the other side, letting go of each other's hands and ducking, though that wouldn't do much since they were walking across an open yard. Stepping out of the pool of light from the streetlight was a relief. Cassie made a beeline for Sheila's garage, Antonio right behind her. They pressed themselves against the side of the building and looked around. A light had come on in the house across the street, but it went out a moment later. She didn't see any other signs that anyone was investigating the noise of Verity driving away.

"Shoot, I forgot to bring a flashlight," Antonio muttered from beside her.

She turned to look at him and had to fight back the urge to giggle madly. They were utterly terrible at this. "We can use our phones, right?"

"I guess that'll work."

She inched over to the garage window and pressed the back of her phone against it, then turned the flashlight on, pressing her face to the glass to peer inside. Sure enough, there was an older sedan parked in the dark building. She squinted, trying to make out the lines of the vehicle. Her phone's light wasn't very strong, and Antonio's wasn't much better.

"Look, I think the back bumper is crushed in," he said.

"Is it? Are you sure it's not just a shadow?"

He sighed, turning off his phone's light and looking around again. "I wish there was a better angle to see from."

She hesitated, then walked over to the garage door —not the overhead door, but the one on the side of the building that opened to where the garbage bin was kept. She looked at Antonio, then reached for the doorknob and tried it. It turned without resistance.

They exchanged another look, a silent question going between them. Were they really going to do this? But she had to admit, there did seem to be something wrong with the vehicle's back bumper. And the way Sheila had acted, the way she'd watched them through her window after the dinner... It definitely had caused alarm bells to go off in her head.

She took a deep breath and turned the doorknob the rest of the way, pushing the door open. It didn't make a sound, and she stepped into the dark garage, Antonio hurrying to follow behind her. He shut the door quietly, and Cassie turned on her phone's flashlight again, cupping her hand around it so the light wouldn't be too obvious through the window. They walked through the garage, which was one of the cleanest Cassie had seen, and around to the back of the vehicle. There, in the stark light from her phone's flashlight, she saw an obvious dent in the vehicle's back bumper.

"Wow," she breathed. "I ... I wasn't actually expecting to find anything."

"What do we do now? Should we call the police?"

"Maybe? How would we explain how we found

this, though? We decided we weren't actually going to break in, but … we kind of just did."

"We could just say we saw it through the window."

"I don't want to lie to the police," Cassie said. "Maybe … maybe I could contact Ellie about it, and she could find a way to say something. She'd have an actual, plausible reason to come over to Sheila's house. Or her grandmother would."

"I can't believe this old lady really killed that poor woman," Antonio breathed. "I mean, I know I'd said that I thought it was possible, but it just seems so unbelievable. This is real."

Cassie frowned at the car, staring at the vehicle's damage.

"I don't know. I mean, I don't know if she did. I know it seems pretty suspicious in light of everything else, but how on earth would she have backed into Ryanne hard enough to kill her? Her body was found outside of the condo complex on the main road. Sheila would've had to have been backing up along the road pretty fast for that to happen, and I just can't think of a reason why she would be doing that."

"What else could it be?" Antonio asked quietly. "Why else would she try to hide this damage to her car?"

Cassie was trying to come up with a reasonable answer when the door that led between the garage and the condo opened, spilling light across them. They both looked up to see Sheila, dressed in a bathrobe and holding a cane up threateningly, staring at them with wide eyes.

CHAPTER THIRTEEN

"Who are you? What are you doing here?"

Cassie took a step back, her shoulder brushing Antonio's. Her heart was in her throat as the other woman's eyes squinted.

"I know you. You were over at Ann's house the other day, weren't you? You work for her granddaughter."

The accusation and recognition in the woman's voice made Cassie feel like she was going to throw up.

"I–I–"

The sound of breaking glass made all three of them jump. Cassie turned, her eyes wide, but the sound had come from outside. When she looked back at Sheila, the other woman's lips were pressed in a thin, angry line. "Is someone else here? What are you doing here?"

"It's just us," Cassie said quickly. "I don't know what that was."

"Why are you in my garage?"

"What happened to your car?" Antonio countered. The question seemed to take Sheila by surprise. She blinked, her gaze going to her vehicle.

"That's none of your business, young man. I'm going to call the police. We'll let them sort this out. None of you move a muscle."

A shout from outside made Cassie jump again, and she realized that something was going on—something that had nothing to do with them and Sheila. She took one last look at the woman's angry face, then glanced at Antonio. He met her eyes, and she glanced toward the door, raising her eyebrows. He nodded fractionally. Then, the two of them turned and ran. She could hear Sheila yelling angrily behind them, but they ignored her. The sound of breaking glass and that shout had her more concerned.

They rounded the corner to find themselves in Sheila's backyard. It led directly to Nonna's yard. There was a knee-high plastic white fence dividing the stretches of grass, and on the other side, in Nonna's yard, a shadowy form was struggling on the porch. No—two shadowy forms, one struggling with the other.

Cassie's phone's flashlight was still on, and she belatedly raised the device to try to see what was going on. The sliding glass door to Nonna's porch had been shattered, and someone wearing all black with a ski mask tugged over their face was struggling with Ellie. Ellie, who was in her pajamas, was trying to fight off the person who had a hand over her mouth to no avail.

"Hey!" Antonio called out, jumping over the knee-high fence. "Let her go!"

Cassie hurried to follow him, jumping over the fence and running toward the struggle. As she neared the house, she saw Nonna standing in her kitchen, her hands pressed to her mouth as she watched in horror through the shattered door. The person who was struggling with Ellie backed away, dragging Ellie with him and keeping his hand pressed over her mouth.

"Let go of her right now," Antonio said, slowing as he neared them. "I mean it—"

"He has a knife," Cassie gasped, spotting the gleam of the metal where it was pressed against Ellie's ribs.

"Please, help her," Nonna begged from inside.

Cassie came to a stop next to Antonio, watching the figure struggling with Ellie and feeling helpless. What was going on? Who was that man? She could tell it was a man from his build and his height. Whoever it was had to be muscular, they probably worked a physical job—

Then she remembered the groundskeeper's truck that had been parked in the clubhouse parking lot. She felt like an idiot. Hadn't Bridget mentioned him as a possible suspect just days ago?

"Evan?" she ventured. "Antonio, it's the groundskeeper."

The figure froze, and she knew she was right. Nonna made a noise of surprise from where she was standing in the kitchen, keeping her bare feet back from the broken glass. "Evan? I don't understand. Why would he want to hurt Ellie?"

Cassie's mind was blank too, until a single sentence she'd heard a week ago came back to her. *When did you get a new truck, Evan?*

"He—I think he killed her. Ryanne Dallas, I mean."

The man froze at that. His distraction was enough that Ellie had a chance to drive her elbow into his stomach. He grunted and loosened his grip enough for her to pull away. She stumbled away from him, breathing air in in ragged gasps.

"Cassie—what are you *doing* here?"

"It's ... a long story. I don't understand. Why would he kill her?"

The man tore the ski mask off his face, which was contorted in anger. She had been right. It was Evan, but the good-natured groundskeeper she'd met before was almost unrecognizable. He looked insane.

"I know why," Nonna said before he could speak. "They were going to replace him when they sold the retirement community. That was part of the plan Ryanne had for improving this place. I remember reading about it in the newsletter. They were going to hire a professional team to do the landscaping. That's why you did it, isn't it? All of this over a job."

Evan glared at each of them in turn, seeming unable to decide who to focus on. "I've been working here for *years*. I've given this place everything. I know every blade of grass like the back of my hand. They were going to drop me like all the years I've spent working here meant nothing. And don't act like you weren't glad when that lady turned up dead. No one wanted her to buy this place out. It was my livelihood, and it's your home that were at stake."

"No one wanted her *dead*," Ellie said, backing

away until she was standing near Antonio and Cassie. "You murdered her. No job is worth someone's life."

"It wasn't—I didn't plan on it," Evan said, his fingers tightening on the knife. There was a desperate look in his eyes. "I was leaving for the day when I saw her standing out on the road, taking pictures of the entrance. I don't remember making a choice. My foot pressed down on the gas pedal, and before I knew it, her body was in the ditch, and I was driving away. I didn't even realize my truck had a dent in it until I got home."

"That's why you had a new one," Ellie said. "I should have guessed when Sheila mentioned you got a new one. I thought it was, well…" She trailed off, looking at Nonna with an apology in her eyes. "I thought it was Sheila."

"We thought it was Sheila too," Cassie admitted to her boss.

"Why was he attacking you?" Antonio asked, glancing between Ellie and Evan.

She frowned, but before anyone else could talk, Nonna stepped forward, carefully avoiding the broken glass, and picked up a bag that someone must have dropped on the porch when the glass shattered. Cassie wondered if Evan had been trying to break in, or if it had broken in the struggle with Ellie. "What's this?"

Everyone watched as she opened it and took out a plastic baggie with some pills inside and a folded piece of paper. She unfolded the paper and read it quickly, her expression turning horrified.

"It's...it's a note. It's not your handwriting, Ellie, but someone signed your name on it. It's a confession about killing Ryanne and—and—" She broke off. "Oh, it's too horrible to say."

"It's a suicide note, isn't it?" Ellie asked, sounding horrified as she turned back to Evan. "You were trying to pin the murder on me."

Evan shifted, looking between them. He looked torn between running away and trying his best to kill them all. "The police were getting too close," he said. "They were asking questions about why I sold my old truck when I did. I had to do something to get them off my trail. It was nothing personal."

"Why don't you put the knife down?" Antonio suggested, stepping forward. "There are too many witnesses here. There's nothing you can do."

Evan took a step back, the trapped, terrified expression on his face only growing in intensity. "No. It can't be over. I'm not going to prison."

He took another step back, then turned to flee. Antonio took a step after him as if he was going to give chase, but Cassie lunged forward and grabbed his arm. Evan still had that knife. "No, don't risk getting hurt," she said. "He's dangerous."

"The police are on their way!"

All of them turned at the sound of the voice coming from the yard behind Cassie to see Sheila running through the grass, wearing fuzzy slippers on her feet and with her bathrobe flying up behind her. "I called them, and they're going to get to the bottom of this. You hooligans aren't going to get away with—" She froze, staring in shock at the scene with all of them gathered in Nonna's yard. Belatedly, Nonna turned on the porch light, which illuminated the broken glass. "What's going on?"

"Sheila?" Nonna said. "What are you doing? You said the police are on their way?"

"These two just broke into my garage," Sheila said, pointing at Cassie and Antonio.

"Cassie, what's going on?" Ellie asked.

This whole night had turned into a nightmare, and it was just getting worse. Cassie gave her boss an embarrassed smile.

"Well, you see, we thought we might be able to solve the murder on our own…"

EPILOGUE

That night was possibly the longest night of Cassie's life. The police showed up soon after they had migrated inside, and they all gave their statements. Thankfully, after hearing the full story, Sheila agreed not to press any charges against Cassie and Antonio. Then they waited, nervously, in Nonna's kitchen. Cassie and Ellie swept up the broken glass while Antonio managed to temporarily patch the broken door with a tarp Nonna had in her garage. Ellie kept shooting narrow-eyed glances at Sheila, but didn't confront her until they were done cleaning up.

"You're the one who damaged my rental car," she said as she took a seat at the table, her voice full of realization. "That's how the damage to my bumper happened. You backed into it."

"It was an accident," Sheila promised, wringing her hands. "I felt horrible."

"Why would you hide it?" Nonna asked from where she was sitting next to Ellie. She kept looking her granddaughter over, as if not daring to believe that she was really okay. Now, she focused on her friend, confusion evident in her expression.

"I'm afraid that they'll take away my license if I get any more marks on my record," Sheila said. "I know I should've let you claim the insurance, but I can't stop driving, I just can't. I don't know what I'd do without that freedom."

Ellie frowned. Cassie didn't blame her; without an incident report, she would probably have to pay for repairs herself. Nonna looked at Sheila sadly.

"Sheila, dear, you can't keep quiet about this. You know it's not right."

"I know." The older woman sighed, looking down at the table. "I'll contact my insurance company in the morning. I apologize for causing you trouble, Ellie. I should have been honest about what happened from the start. I can't blame these two for thinking I was hiding something. I was, just not what they thought."

"Sorry if we scared you," Cassie said. It seemed like it was time for apologies all around. "Antonio and I shouldn't have gone into your garage like that.

We thought something strange was going on, but we were just going to look in through the window. My curiosity got the better of me."

"It all turned out all right in the end," Nonna said, patting Ellie's hand and smiling at the others. "Now, who wants tea?"

They waited for hours to hear if Evan had been arrested. They finally got the call early in the morning. He'd been caught and had been taken in. The news was a relief to all of them. Cassie could tell that Ellie was still shaken by what had happened. Even though they had swept up the glass from the broken door and covered it up, she kept glancing over at the tarp, her face pale. Finally, Cassie realized that it was time for her to go. It would be dawn soon, and she was dead on her feet.

"I think Antonio and I should head back to town," she said. "I just want to apologize again, for everything."

"You don't need to apologize," Ellie assured her, rising to her feet. "You probably saved my life." She gave them an almost wistful smile. "And ... I'd be a hypocrite if I blamed you for doing something I would have done. You should listen to some of the stories my husband has to tell about me. You remind me of myself."

"You'll have to tell me some of them sometime," Cassie said, exchanging a smile with her boss. Ellie smiled back at her, and she knew that everything would be all right. Ellie wasn't mad, and Evan would be going to prison. Verity was the last loose end. Hopefully, when she heard that someone had been arrested for Ryanne's murder, she would be able to find some sort of closure … and would stop stalking Ellie now that she would have proof she wasn't the killer.

"I will. Remind me next time we talk. Though, I'd appreciate it if you didn't pass the stories on to the employees. I've got to keep up some sort of reputation."

Cassie laughed and agreed to keep stories of Ellie's wilder adventures a secret, then hugged her boss goodbye before she and Antonio left. After all the commotion, the walk back to where his SUV was parked seemed quiet. When they finally got into the vehicle and he started the engine, she looked over at him.

"I hate to say this, but I think the next time you want to do something like this, the answer is going to be no. I much preferred bowling."

He nodded in agreement and pulled out of the

parking lot. "So did I. We'll stick with something a bit tamer for our next date."

She grinned as they turned onto the road. It *had* been a date, after all.